ALLERGIC TO THE GREAT WALL, THE FORBIDDEN PALACE, AND OTHER TOURIST ATTRACTIONS

ALVIN HO

ALLERGIC TO THE GREAT WALL, THE FORBIDDEN PALACE, AND OTHER TOURIST ATTRACTIONS

BY Lenore LOOK   PICTURES BY LeUyen Pham

A YEARLING BOOK

Text copyright © 2014 by Lenore Look
Cover art and interior illustrations copyright © 2014 by LeUyen Pham

All rights reserved. Published in the United States by Yearling, an imprint of Random House Children's Books, a division of Penguin Random House LLC, New York. Originally published in hardcover in the United States by Schwartz & Wade Books, an imprint of Random House Children's Books, New York, in 2013.

Yearling and the jumping horse design are registered trademarks of Penguin Random House LLC.

Visit us on the Web! randomhousekids.com

Educators and librarians, for a variety of teaching tools, visit us at RHTeachersLibrarians.com

The Library of Congress has cataloged the hardcover edition of this work as follows:
Look, Lenore.
Alvin Ho : allergic to the Great Wall, the Forbidden Palace, and other tourist attractions / by Lenore Look ; pictures by LeUyen Pham. — First edition.
pages cm
Summary: Fearful seven-year-old Alvin Ho goes on a trip to China with his family.
ISBN 978-0-385-36972-5 (hc) — ISBN 978-0-385-36973-2 (glb) —
ISBN 978-0-449-81986-9 (ebook)
[1. Fear—Fiction. 2. Travel—Fiction. 3. Chinese Americans—Fiction.
4. China—Fiction.] I. Pham, LeUyen, illustrator. II. Title.
PZ7.L8682Ap 2014
[Fic]—dc23
2013033324

ISBN 978-0-553-52055-2 (pbk.)

Printed in the United States of America
10 9 8 7 6 5 4
First Yearling Edition 2015

This book belongs to Katie and Claire Stromseth,
who climbed the Great Wall with me.
—L.L.

To Sabrina, who loves visiting China.
—L.P.

AUTHOR'S ACKNOWLEDGMENTS

This book required a month of travel and research in China. I met many remarkable people along the way who dropped everything to help me and to make me feel at home. It's impossible to fit all my (and Alvin's) wonderful (and sometimes scary) adventures into one book, but I do wish to thank all those who shared the journey with me. Among them are:

Lisa Bow and Jonathan Stromseth, for their amazing hospitality in Beijing.

Pan Wei Bing, for driving me all over Shandong Province so that I could see the largest dinosaur pit in the world and Confucius's birthplace (not the same location).

Shi Yan Chen and all my monk brothers at Shaolin Temple in Henan Province, for teaching me kung fu and treating me as one of their own.

Guo Nai Xiang and Wang Dan, for their warmest hospitality in Wangzigou.

Liao Wo Zhang, Zhou Wan Wen, Liao Zi Xin, and Sylvia Liao, for their generous hospitality in Guangzhou.

Angela Bow, Jean-Claude Humair, and their girls, Alexandra and Isabelle, for their gracious hospitality in Hong Kong.

And as always, many thanks to the Phamtastic LeUyen Pham and the Amazing Annie Kelley, for being there for Alvin from beginning to end.

CHAPTER ONE

Airport Security

the name on the passport said Alvin Ho.

That's my name, all right.

But the photo looked nothing like me.

Not one bit.

When you're a handsome dude like me, but your photo looks like you just robbed a bank and got run over by the getaway car, it's enough to scare the flickering headlights out of you.

And I'm already scared of many things.

Emergency exits.

Emergency landings.

Oxygen masks.

Seat cushions that are also life preservers.

Toilets that are also exits.

Recycled air.

Strangers.

Small enclosed spaces.

Small enclosed spaces filled with strangers, hurtling across the sky at 600 miles per hour, 36,000 feet in the air. That's almost two miles above the peak of Mount Everest!

Thin air.

I was born scared, and I'm still scared, and that's the way it's going to be, my brother Calvin says, until I'm a man. Then I'll be bigger and scared of bigger things.

Gulp.

What's bigger than an entire continent? My passport was being swiped through a machine at the airport. It was winter break, and we were—gasp!—GOING TO CHINA!!!!

It was not a good idea.

In fact, it was a really horrible idea.

China, as everyone knows, is on the other side of the world, where everything is upside down and a day ahead of us.

Worse, we had a new baby in our family, Baby Claire, who's a girl, and who's no bigger than a fish, and my mom and dad were planning to show her off to relatives in China.

Imagine showing off a salmon, while standing upside down, on a day that hasn't happened yet. What could be scarier than that???!!!!

Nothing.

Except for the plane ride. First you get on. Then you die. You can't go to China the regular way anymore, by digging a hole. There are too many underground cables and dead bodies, not like it was in the old days, when there were no cables and just a few dead bodies.

Now we were in line in front of the sign that said SECURITY CHECKPOINT. It was a long, snaky line, that's for sure.

I stood on one foot.

Then I stood on the other.

"Oh, Alvin," my mom said.

Oh no. When she says "Oh, Alvin" like that, it's not good news. Especially when going to the bathroom means you'll have to come back and stand at the end of the line all over again.

But my mom knows that when you gotta go, you gotta go.

I couldn't help it!

My dad said our plane would fly for sixteen hours nonstop. No way I could hold it for that long! I know better than to use the airplane toilets with the powerful sucking action. Ever notice how full the plane is at takeoff and then wonder why there are empty seats during the flight? Well, now you know.

"C'mon," my dad sighed. "We should all go."

So we did. All of us: Mom, Dad, Calvin, Anibelly and me. Baby Claire was in her carrier on Dad's chest and doesn't go to the bathroom the regular way, but she came along anyway.

After that, I felt much better. Everything was

fine and the line was moving even slower than
before, which was okay on account of the slower
it moved, the longer we were alive. We were almost at the place where people were taking off
their clothes and shoes to be x-rayed, when . . .

Gasp!

I stopped dead in my tracks.

"What's the matter now?" my dad asked.

My eyes popped.

My mouth opened.

But nothing came out.

"His PDK is missing," Calvin said. "He's not
carrying his Personal Disaster Kit."

Calvin's nine and he's very helpful. Usually

he's kicking my butt, but he can also tell what's wrong with me.

"Maybe you left it in the bathroom," Anibelly said. She's four. But she can figure things out like she's six or something.

Oops.

So my dad and I left the line again.

And went back to the bathroom.

It was a good thing we did—my PDK was right there in the stall where I had set it down. TGIDLLASP—Thank God It Didn't Look Like A Suspicious Package!

Then the mackerel needed to be changed. That's the thing about babies—they need to be changed all the time. Lucky for her, we were already in the bathroom.

After that, we waited at the end of the line again. Calvin, Anibelly and my mom were already on the other side of the checkpoint, waiting for us.

Eventually, my dad and I got back to the place where everyone was taking off their shoes and clothes and throwing them into bins as fast as they could. I love taking off my clothes! Normally, my clothes come off, just like that. But this was not normal.

I was wearing *all* my clothes and had packed none of them. When you travel, the important thing, as everyone knows, is to have room in your suitcase for souvenir candy. But the problem with wearing all your clothes is that you have to take them all off. They won't even let you leave on a belt.

Those are the rules.

Lucky me, I figured out how to strip off nine layers of T-shirts all at once, so I was undressed, just like that.

"Alvin's naked!" I heard Anibelly shriek.

My mom gasped.

Her eyes popped.

Her jaw dropped.

Oops. Was I *not* supposed to get naked?

But it was too late.

All my clothes had disappeared into the X-ray machine. There was nothing I could do but stand there like tofu without sauce.

Suddenly, security police hurried over as my PDK was coming out of the X-ray machine, and they grabbed it!

I froze.

"Whose bag is this?" a voice boomed.

Security cameras pointed at me.

"It's my son's . . . ," my dad said.

"Where's your son?"

My dad turned.

His eyes popped.

His mouth opened.

But nothing came out.

Normally, this doesn't happen to him. He always has something to say to me, or he might curse a blue streak like William Shakespeare if he's trying very hard to be a gentleman.

But this was not normal. I was naked, but my PDK was not. Out came: sunscreen, sports drinks, all sorts of forks and knives (I'm allergic to chopsticks), cheese (my favorite snack, hard to

find in China), a mirror, bug spray, a lighter, lighter fluid, rope (for climbing the Great Wall), a face mask (Chinese superstition says that if you breathe smog, you will die), escape plans.

I had spent hours packing my PDK the night before. I had no idea what I needed for China, but Calvin and Anibelly helped me figure it out.

"I NEED MY PDK!!!" I wanted to scream. But it was too late.

"Please step aside, sir," someone said to my dad. "We need to ask you a few questions."

CHAPTER TWO
Air Safety

getting through airport security was not easy for my dad.

By the time they let him go, he looked like he'd already been on va-cation for a week! Nor-mally, vacation is very stressful for my dad. But this was not nor-mal. We hadn't even gotten on our plane yet.

My poor dad.

But there was no time to feel sorry for him. We had to make a mad dash to the gate. We nearly missed our plane!

Getting on the plane was not easy for me.

In fact, it was nearly almost *impossible.*

My entire family rolled right in like rocks into a ditch.

But I stopped dead in my tracks just inches from the door.

The good news was that I could grip the side of the plane really well. I've had lots of practice.

The bad news was that my dad came back for me and turned me into carry-on luggage, just like that.

Poor me.

But poor Calvin too. As soon as the plane started to pull away from the gate, Calvin got sick.

Super-duper sick.

Calvin's like that. He's a scientist, an inventor, an explorer, a Boy Scout, and a karate chopper-upper—but he's not an astronaut. He gets moving sickness on a plane as soon as it backs away from the gate, every time.

Poor Calvin.

He had to close his eyes.

But poor me too.

Calvin had gotten sick on *me*. My pants, which I'd had a hard time getting back on after passing through security, were now completely ruined. But lucky me, I had on several other pairs underneath those. Wearing all my clothes was very useful!

"Oh, Alvin," my mom said. "Aren't you terribly warm?"

I blinked.

I scratched.

I had so many itches I couldn't reach!

And yes, I was kind of warm, now that she mentioned it.

But it was time for takeoff, and there are rules for takeoff:

```
RULES FOR TAKEOFF

1. All seats in their full and uptight position.
2. All tray tables locked away.
3. All electronic equipment turned off.
4. All clothes kept on.
5. Fasten your seat belt.
6. Note emergency exits.
7. In case of an emergency, put the oxygen
   mask on yourself first before you
   help your child.
```

Whaaaaat???

The plane loudened.

My face flattened.

I got sucked into my seat. *Sluuuuurp!*

Faster and faster we went.

Louder and louder it got.

Then suddenly, we plunged into the air like a
diver into water, only upward—toward the sun—
and zoomed up, just like that.

"Son," my dad said.

I stopped.

"Isn't that enough hand sanitizer?"

> **HOW TO SURVIVE A 16-HOUR FLIGHT**
> 1. Be on high alert.
> 2. Ask your mom for antibacterial hand sanitizer.
> 3. Rub it on.
> 4. Rub on more.
> 5. Just rub it on!

I looked at the bottle.

"It's my best friend, Dad," I said. "And it should be yours too."

I squeezed a little into my dad's palm, but not too much.

The problem with being locked in a plane, as everyone knows, is that the germs can kill you. A small enclosed tube where hundreds of people breathe the same air for sixteen hours is a death trap! Viruses! Fungi! Bacteria! Recycled air makes you tired. Then it makes you sick. The deadly stuff you can catch from airplane air includes:

Tuberculosis

SARS

Influenza
Measles
Rubella
Diphtheria
Ebola
Smallpox
Anthrax

Calvin had found the list on the Internet and printed it for me.

Lucky for me, I had figured it out. I turned on my air vent. The rush of air, as everyone knows, will push everything away from you. You will not die of airborne illness.

But you could die of deep vein thrombosis.

"Relax," my dad said. "Have a drink."

The drink cart rolled to a stop right in front of us.

My dad got a couple of drinks in tiny bottles.

I got a soda.

In a can.

An *aluminum* can.

The same aluminum that planes are made of.
I *dented* it with my fingernail.

Oops.

Suddenly, I wasn't in a soda mood anymore.

"My throat hurts," I said.

My dad looked at me.

"My left leg looks swollen," I said.

My dad looked at my leg.

"My left lung is collapsed," I said. I know all about collapsed lungs from TV. I clutched my ribs.

My dad clutched me.

"Relax, son," my dad said. "It's a *long* flight."

Then my dad pushed back his seat and closed his eyes. He was very tired.

But I was not. How can you sleep when you're in a flying soda can with several hundred people?

Worse, how do you stay calm when a lady

suddenly appears out of nowhere and is smiling at you?

"Welcome aboard, sir," she said.

I blinked.

When you're a gentleman and a lady talks to you for no good reason, you shouldn't duck under the seat in front of you even if you want to. It's one of the rules of being a gentleman, I think. I'm not exactly sure. I can't remember.

"You must be the junior pilot," she said.

Then she pressed a pair of shiny wings on my chest.

The junior what???

But there they were—a pair of genuine gold pilot wings.

What was I supposed to do with those? Fly the plane?

Was something wrong with the pilot?

Was this an *emergency*???

"Dad," I said.

"Uhhh," my dad grunted.

"I'm the junior pilot," I said.

"God," my dad said. His head dropped.

Was my dad praying? Or did he mean to say "good"? It was hard to tell.

"Dad," I said, giving him a shove. "What do I do?"

"Keep . . . it . . . horizontal," my dad said. His eyes were still closed.

Keep it horizontal???!!!!

I looked over at Calvin. He reads a lot. He always knows what to do. But his eyes were closed too.

And my mom and Anibelly and the halibut, their eyes were closed.

I looked around.

Most people had their eyes closed. It was very quiet on the plane.

I'd read about this.

Normal people can't stand g-forces and pass out.

That meant I was not normal.

I was special.

I was the junior pilot.

"Ladies and gentlemen," a voice said, "the

captain has turned on the seat belt sign. Please return to your seats and fasten your seat belts."

"This is your captain speaking," another voice said. "We'll be experiencing some turbulence ahead. It'll be a little rough until we rise above the storm. There will be no cabin service at this time. Flight attendants, please take your seats."

Turbulence?

Storm?

Flying even higher?

What was a junior pilot supposed to do?

Ruuumble. Ruuumble.

The plane shook.

Then it rattled.

The lights went out.

Everything went up and down.

Creeeak. Creeeak.

It sounded like the plane was coming apart!

Was that why they made me the junior pilot?

In case I survived and the pilot didn't???

"Dad!" I said. "We're going to DIE!!!"

Silence.

My dad was fast asleep. All the dudes in my family fall asleep just like that. And they stay asleep. Except for me. I'm on high alert all the time.

And anyone on high alert could see that we needed our oxygen masks and floatation devices, for sure! (I had watched the emergency video.)

So I pushed the call button for help.

Nothing.

I pushed my dad's call button for help.

It lit up.

I pushed my dad.

Nothing.

I pushed him again.

Nothing.

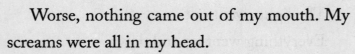

Worse, nothing came out of my mouth. My screams were all in my head.

That's the thing with me. When I'm all freaked out, I can't make a sound. I can't speak, I can't grunt, I can't howl, I can't even cry. I'm as silent as air in a can.

But my dad's red call button was not.

It chimed for help every time I pushed it.

So I pushed it eight sqillion times.

CHAPTER THREE

Not in Concord Anymore

my dad was so busted.

I'd never seen a federal air marshal before, but I've seen one now. TWO, to be exact.

An air marshal, as everyone knows, is a plainclothes officer who flies in planes to keep an eye on things, just in case. Usually, you'd never know they're on board. They blend in. They look like regular passengers.

How my dad explained pushing his call button like a maniac during a storm with no cabin service, I have no idea. The marshals took him in the back to question him in private.

My poor dad.

But poor me too, when my dad came back to his seat.

"Wherefore art thou such a jumpy, multilayered, overdressed, bootless button pusher?" my dad said. The expression on his face said that if I so much as *looked* at the call button again, I'd have another thing coming, and it wouldn't be the nice lady or the not-so-nice air marshals.

"Son," my dad said firmly. "We have another thirteen hours on the flight. I would strongly suggest . . ."

Thirteen hours???!!! Isn't that a bad-luck number?

Whatever else my dad said, I have no idea.

How were we ever going to survive thirteen hours of bad luck???

•●•●•

That night I had a super-duper scary dream. I dreamt that I got on a plane with emergency exits and oxygen masks and toilets that could suck you into outer space and woke up in a foreign movie with no subtitles.

"*Ni hao,*" my dad said.

"*Wo hao,*" said Anibelly.

"*Ni eh ma?*" my mom asked.

"*Wo hen eh!*" Calvin said.

They sounded like a real Chinese family speaking real Chinese in a real Chinese restaurant. I've always wanted to do that! So I opened my mouth, but nothing came out. Worse, we were sitting around with a bunch of relatives who sounded like they'd all been to Chinese school.

Then they all started eating with chopsticks, even Anibelly. She was never good with

chopsticks, but now she looked like she'd been born with 'em! When did she learn to use chopsticks like that???

I'm allergic to chopsticks.

I wasn't eating at all.

The only other person who couldn't use chopsticks was the tuna. And she's a baby.

It didn't look good.

For me.

I tossed.

I turned.

I wrestled with an alien.

I hung on for dear life from a UFO.

I turned into a dim sum.

"Alvin," said a voice from above.

Chopsticks pinched me and pulled me from my steam-basket grave.

The chopsticks of God. I was sure of it.

I blinked.

My dad blinked back.

I love seeing my dad. I can be freaking out, but as soon as I see my dad, I'm okay.

"Son," he said.

"Dad?"

"You were having a bad dream," he whispered.

I nodded. I clutched my blanket. My dad clutched me.

I love it when he does that. I love it more than Legos.

"I dreamt you were speaking in Chinese," I said. "I dreamt everyone was speaking in Chinese. Everyone but me."

My dad chuckled.

"You were a *real* Chinese dude!" I said. "There were no pictures on the menu!"

"Hmmm," said my dad.

"I also dreamt that I was in an airplane with emergency exits and oxygen masks and hungry toilets, for a longlonglong time," I said. "We were all going to die and no one knew it on account of everyone was watching movies and not paying attention, except for me—I was the only one keeping an eye on things and I needed to make a parachute, fast!"

Silence.

"Is that why you were tying Claire's blankets together?" my dad asked.

I looked down. I was still clutching a little baby blanket.

How did my dad know what happened in my dream?

My eyes grew big and round.

And when my eyes are like that, I can see a lot of things.

My room was kind of strange.

Everyone was asleep. Normally, it's only me and Calvin in my room. But this was not normal. Even the Chilean sea bass, who sleeps in my mom and dad's room in a special bed called a bass-in-net (on account of that's what she is), was in my room.

Calvin was there in his usual place, but Lucy, my dog, was not. Instead, Anibelly was there, curled next to my mom.

It was really strange.

Come to think of it, it didn't look like my room at all.

Or did it?

I rubbed my eyes.

I clutched my blanket.

Huh? Was this my blanket?

"Dad?"

"Son," he said, breathing heavily.

"Am I still dreaming?"

"You have jet lag," my dad said. "It's not time to get up yet."

"What's a jet leg?" I asked, grabbing my leg. "Is that a disease?"

"Jet lag is . . . ," my dad said. ZZZZzzzzzz.

"Dad!" I said. "Why does my room look so funny?"

"It's not your room, son," my dad said.

"It's not?"

"We're at our relatives'," my dad said. "Don't you remember?"

"No."

"It was a long flight," my dad said. "I wish I didn't remember either."

A long flight?

Relatives?

"Where are we?" I asked.

ZZZZzzzzzzzzzzzz.

"Dad, where are we???" I asked again.

"Beijing," said my sleepy dad.

"You mean Back Bay?" I asked.

My dad breathed in.

My dad breathed out.

My dad's like that in the mornings. He sputters like an old car starting up on a cold day. Lots of exhaust, but going nowhere.

"No," my dad said. "Beijing. The . . . the capital of . . ."

ZZZzzzzzzzzzzzzzz.

"Of what?" I cried.

"China."

CHINA???

"We're all exhausted," my dad said. "You nodded off during dinner last night. We'll go on a tour when we get up."

But I *was* up.

"You mean we're not in Concord anymore???" I asked.

I popped out of bed and hurried to the window.

Eeeeeeeeek!

I was up in the sky like a bird! It was gray and

foggy. Buildings below looked like toy houses. Cars looked like ants.

"THIS IS CHINA?"

I did not feel well.

I have acrophobia.

"Shhh," said my dad. "You'll wake the baby."

"IS THIS REALLY CHINA??? BUT IT LOOKS SO NORMAL. NOTHING'S UP-SIDE DOWN!!!"

"Wah!" cried the bass-in-net. *"WAAAAAAAA-AAAAAAAAAH!"*

CHAPTER FOUR

Allergic to China

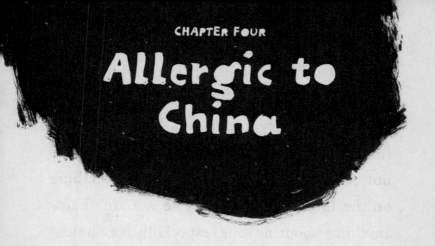

the worst thing about being in China was everything.

The baby was howling.

The toilet was crying.

Anibelly was singing "Lalalalalalala" and dancing along with the stars on Chinese TV.

She was the only one in a good mood.

My dad looked like a used tea bag.

My mom looked like loose tea leaves.

And Calvin was grumpy grumpy grumpy.

"You're the first person to land in China and not know it," Calvin said. "It's a good thing you're not named Marco Polo."

Calvin is very smart, but he wasn't born that way. He has to read everything. When he's not reading a book, he's reading something on the Internet. Otherwise, he wouldn't know anything about anyone, especially famous explorers like Marco Polo, Xuanzang, Zheng He and Fa Xian.

"You're like a piece of luggage," Calvin said. "*Excess* luggage."

He was grumpy that the sturgeon woke him up with her crying on account of I woke her up with my screaming. And Calvin loves to sleep.

"You don't pay attention," Calvin continued. "You're never going to be a brave explorer like me. You don't know where you're going, you don't know where you've been, and you don't know where you are."

I knew where we were.

We were in our relatives' house on the thirty-second floor!

The air was unbreatheable. You had to stand next to the air-purifying machine, or else!

The water was undrinkable. You couldn't brush your teeth with it. You couldn't have ice cubes.

You had to use bottled water. Or boiled water. But you still had to shower.

And you had to keep your mouth shut tight while showering, or else!

This is what it's like on the other side of the world, ten sqillion miles from home, in the birthplace of more than a billion people (alive), and the burial place of an army of creepy clay soldiers (dead), and where EARTHQUAKES happen all the time.

Worse, I had to meet the relatives. They all knew me, but I didn't know them. How does that always happen?

HOW TO MEET YOUR RELATIVES (AGAIN!)

1. Stand behind your mom.
2. Clutch her leg.
3. Just clutch her leg.
4. Keep clutching her leg.

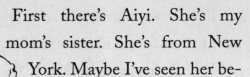

First there's Aiyi. She's my mom's sister. She's from New York. Maybe I've seen her before and maybe I haven't. It's hard to say. She's very nice.

Then there's Uncle Jonathan. He doesn't look Chinese at all. He looks plain. But he speaks better Chinese than anyone. He's a gentleman, like my dad, you can tell.

Then there are my cousins.

Katie. She's Calvin's age. They were friends just like that.

And Bean Sprout. She's about the same size as Anibelly. She's a girl. And girls, as everyone knows, are annoying.

"AlvinAlvinAlvinAlvinAlvin," she sang as she hip-hopped. "AlvinAlvinAlvinAlvin."

Shimmy, shimmy.

Shake, shake.

Ooh. Why do I always get the girl???

She was worse than Anibelly!

"You are my sunshine, AlvinAlvin," she rapped. "My only sunshine, you make me happy when skies are gray!"

The skies were gray, all right.

I thought my Chinese relatives were going to be *real* Chinese who spoke only Chinese and didn't know any English. At least, they were like that in my dream. I was really disappointed.

•●•●•

Breakfast was not what I had expected either.

It was not breakfast.

It was dinner.

There were noodles—fat noodles, flat noodles, skinny noodles, fried noodles. Plain rice. Fried rice. Congee. Green beans. Red pepper. Yellow squash. Pumpkin soup. Meat kebabs. Hot dogs. Steamed buns. Steamed soy milk. Salted duck eggs. Salted fish. Potstickers. Tofu.

"Our maid prepared a typical Chinese breakfast to welcome you," Aiyi said.

"Everything looks delicious," my mom said.

"Everything is scrumptious," Uncle Jonathan said. "The Chinese eat big breakfasts. You'd better get used to it."

"I'm already used to it," Calvin said, piling it on.

"It's the perfect start to a busy day of sightseeing," my dad added. He piled it on too.

Everyone filled their plates except me.

"Oh, Alvin," my mom said. "Aren't you hungry?"

I blinked.

My sad reflection blinked back at me from the plate.

"I don't think he wants to have dinner for breakfast," Katie said helpfully. "I was like that when I first moved to Beijing."

"Not me!" Bean Sprout chirped. "I love dinnerfast!"

"I've always wanted to eat dinner for breakfast too," Calvin said, digging in. He was no longer in a grumpy mood.

But I was.

I like breakfast food for breakfast. And dinner food for dinner.

This was completely upside down!

"Alvin," my mom said, "if you try it, you'll like it."

I didn't want to try it.

I crossed my arms.

I hoped to die.

Well, maybe not that. If I died in a foreign country, I'd have to go home in a body bag. And body bags go in luggage class, where there's no food service.

Grrrrrrr went my stomach.

Urrrrrrr went my liver.

But I said nothing.

What do you say when there's so much food but nothing to eat?

"Son," my dad said firmly, "you're forgetting your manners."

But how do you remember your manners when you're thirty-two floors above the ground on the other side of the world, where the meals are upside down?

And everyone is staring at you?

My mouth opened, but instead of saying "I'm sorry there's nothing good to eat"—Nothing. Came. Out.

My tongue turned to ice.

My words permafrosted to my teeth.

"Oh no!" Anibelly gasped.

"He's allergic to China," Calvin explained. "He can't talk when he's all freaked out about something."

"Oh, Alvin," my mom said. She put her arms around me. She looked very worried.

"We need to be able to hear you in a crowd, son," my dad said. "You could get lost and we won't even know it."

Lost?

In a crowd of more than a billion?

"Maybe he can wear a GPS tracking device," Calvin said. "Like a prisoner."

"Or a leash, like Lucy!" said Anibelly.

"I've got just the thing for you!" Bean Sprout said. She jumped up and dashed into her room. Then she hurried back with a bunch of orange hats in her arms.

"You won't get lost if you wear one of these," Bean Sprout said, passing out destruction-orange hats to everyone—everyone, that is, except me. Mine she slapped on my head.

"All the tourists wear them," she said happily. "All the tour guides carry a little flag." She pulled out a little yellow flag. It did not match our orange caps.

"I'm going to be your tour guide!" Bean Sprout said.

"Just follow me. If you wander off, I'll be able to spot you right away!"

"What a wonderful idea," my mom said.

"Perfect," said my dad.

Bean Sprout smiled. "AlvinAlvinAlvin," she sang as she circled the table in her funny hip-hop. "AlvinAlvinAlvin."

"Lalalalalalala," sang Anibelly, joining her. "Lalalalalala."

Then everyone started talking all at once.

No one said anything more about my manners.

No one remembered that I didn't have any breakfast.

No one that is, except me.

Grrrrrrrrr went my stomach again.

Urrrrrrrrr went my liver.

What's worse than an empty stomach on a cold winter's day?

I looked at my freaked-out reflection in the plate.

An ugly orange hat, that's what!!!

CHAPTER FIVE

Great Wall Facts

sightseeing in beijing is harder than
it looks.

First, you have to check the AQI (Air Quality Index) online. It measures the amount of tiny
particles in the air that can creep deep into your
lungs and make you sick. Any reading over 300
is "hazardous" and everyone is warned to stay indoors. The index tops at 500. Today's reading
was 655!

Second, you need to put together your PDK.

The first thing in your PDK should be the air-purifying machine.

But the problem with the air-purifying machine was that it was bigger than my PDK. *Much* bigger.

Lucky for me, it was on wheels, and I was pushing it out the door when my dad pushed it back in. It was obvious we needed to take one with us. The air outside looked like dirty bathwater!

"Residents in Beijing say that smoking a cigarette is safer than breathing the air," Calvin said, reading from his book *Anyone Can Speak Chinese*, which not only teaches you how to speak Chinese, but also tells you all about China. Calvin had been reading it nonstop for weeks.

"Not to worry," Uncle Jonathan said. "We've learned to schedule our activities around the pollution. Instead of going to the Forbidden City today, we'll drive out to the Great Wall. There's less pollution out there."

"Hooray!" said Katie. "A Great Wall day is a great day!"

"AlvinAlvin," Bean Sprout sang. "You'll love the Great Wall. It's so, so tall. And after you climb it, you can buy a souvenir!"

"I already love it," Calvin said. "And I'm planning to buy a T-shirt that says 'I Climbed the Great Wall.'"

"I want to buy something too!" Anibelly said.

"And I'm looking forward to taking some good pictures," my mom said.

Not me. I didn't want to go anywhere—not if I had to get into an elevator first.

There were thirty-two floors between me and the ground, which meant that it was a terrible way to die if the cables broke and the elevator plunged into a free fall.

So my dad and I took the stairs. No problem. For me. For my dad, there were some is-
sues. His knees are on their last legs. By the
time we got to the bottom, he needed new knees
and hips, and a new attitude, for sure. He was
so cranky!

Then there was the traffic.

The driver's name was Pan. He obeyed all the
signals. He didn't hit any pedestrians. He was
very calm. He does nothing but drive everyone
around every day, Aiyi explained. It's his job.
He's a native Beijinger, so he knows all the streets.
He can read the Chinese street signs. He speaks
only Mandarin.

And he knew his way to the Great Wall at
Mutianyu without a GPS, even though it was
two hours away.

I was very impressed.

And so was Calvin.

"I'm going to be a
Chinese driver when I
grow up," Calvin said.

I nodded. I couldn't

think of a better job either, except for driving a monster truck into a mud hole, which is not something you get to do every day.

The wheels on our minivan went round and round.

The sun came out.

Snow sparkled on the ground.

It was warm and cozy in the car.

I breathed in.

I breathed out.

For the first time since we left home, I felt okay.

"Are we there yet?" I asked.

"Your voice is back!" Anibelly cried. "Hooray!"

"AlvinAlvin!" Bean Sprout sang. "It'll be lunchtime by the time we get there!"

That was good news to me.

But when we finally got there, the sign said "The Schoolhouse."

Huh?

"No one said anything about going to school!!!" I cried.

"It's a restaurant and

art studio," my dad said. "It only used to be a school."

He didn't fool me. Outside, there was a flag on a flagpole, which, as everyone knows, is a sign that school is in session.

So I clung to the tree outside like a panda to a bamboo stalk. My dad couldn't pry me free until he promised that he would take the stairs with me at our relatives' house, every day, no matter what. Up *and* down.

"Fine," my dad said.

"And candy money too," I said. "Every day. Five extra bucks." That was the deal.

Inside the building, I was right—class was in session. People were learning glassblowing. Ovens roared. Tongues of fire hissed and licked at hot molten glass. It was more dangerous and scarier than my own school!

The good news was that lunch was lunch.

It was not breakfast. And it was not dinner. I

had my favorite—a grilled cheese sandwich. And hot chocolate. Yum!

After that, it was time to climb the Great Wall.

"Ready, son?" my dad asked.

I nodded. A grilled cheese sandwich and hot chocolate are magical. I felt ready to climb Mount Everest!

So I hurried after my dad.

Up, up, up the hill we went.

"AlvinAlvin," I heard a little voice behind me.

"Lalalalalalala."

"AlvinAlvinAlvin."

Ooh. Girls are so annoying. Just when I was about to tell them to cut it out, my dad's hands lifted me into something and sat me down.

Bang! The door shut.

We swung just a little; then *whooooooooooo-oshhhhhh,* the wind swept us up into the air.

And I heard the girls no more.

Shhhhhhhhhhhhhhhrrrrrrrrrr. The wind filled my ears.

I blinked.

I was sitting across from my dad, who had the flounder on his chest, in a teeny cable car with plastic windows.

And the cable car was a hundred feet in the air, swinging from a rope by the crook of a tiny steel finger!!!

GASP!!!

How I ever got into this death trap, I have no idea! All I know is that my dad has a history of stepping into traps when he's in the great outdoors.

Higher and higher we went.

Worse, there were many cars like ours dangling from the same rope! Calvin, Katie, Aiyi and Uncle Jonathan were in the one ahead of us. My mom and Anibelly and Bean Sprout were in the one behind us.

And we were all swinging wildly in the wind, high above the pointy treetops. I could see Calvin reading his book and chatting away with Katie as though this were their last day on earth, and I was sure it was!!!

"What a breathtaking view," my dad said. "And look—there's the Great Wall."

I didn't dare move.

Riding a cable car, as everyone knows, is like being in a canoe. Any sudden move or standing up would be the end of us.

So I shifted my eyes without moving my body.

I gasped.

"You know, son," my dad continued, "visiting the Great Wall with my family was near the top of my bucket list."

His bucket list???!!!

I knew all about making a bucket list from my gunggung. It's a list of daring things to do before you die that can kill you before you're dead.

And this was a killer, for sure! I had no idea where the wall was, or what was so great about it. All I saw was a DRAGON!!! Its tail was so thick and long, it whipped and snaked along the mountain's ridge, dipping out of sight here and there, then reappearing, for as far as the eye could see. It was HUMONGOUS!!! Worse, it was so long that I couldn't see its head, which gave me a bad, sinking feeling that it was not the wind rocking our cable car—it was the dragon breathing down our necks!

"AAAAAAAAAAAAAAAAAAAAACK!" I screamed.

But my scream was as silent as the grave. All you could hear was the dragon's breath.

·•·•·

It was a miracle we made it to the top. Was I ever glad when—surprise, surprise—I set my feet on the ground again.

Or was it the ground?

It was not like any ground I'd ever seen before. It was uneven and steep. It was covered with strange scales. Two rows of granite teeth and crenels stuck up like—gasp!—a double-vertebrae spine!

Yikes!

We had landed on top of the dragon's tail!!!
And so had many other people, all of them walking around and taking pictures as though it were
their last day on earth, and I was sure it was!

The dragon had managed to blow much of

the snow off his back, and now he was trying to blow us off too! *Brrrrrr!* It was cold!

The good news was that the sun was out.

The sky was vibrant blue.

The hills were covered with snow.

I blinked.

I never thought I would be so happy to see the sun and the sky. But I was.

The other good news was that Bean Sprout forgot about being a tour guide. She and Anibelly were poking at the dragon's scales and climbing all over the place and talking nonstop in that way that girls do.

The bad news was that Katie was now waving the little flag.

"Welcome to the Great Wall, everyone!" she cried, jumping up and down. "This is my favorite place to visit." Then she bounced up and down some more.

Oooh. I wished she wouldn't do that. The dragon might think she's a mosquito and try to flick her off with a switch of his tail. Then it would be the end of all of us!

"'Construction of the Great Wall started in 221 BC by the emperor Qin Shihuang, who had also built the terra-cotta army to guard his tomb,'" Calvin read from his book. "'The wall was built to keep invaders out.'"

"The average width of the wall is enough for five horsemen or ten soldiers to walk side by side," Katie added.

"And the total length of all its sections is 13,170 miles," Calvin said.

My dad whistled. "That's more than four times the width of the United States," he said.

"'Soldiers defended the wall with crossbows, spears, swords and stones until they invented gunpowder,'" Calvin read. "'From the watchtowers they burned wolf dung and sent smoke signals by day and fire signals by night to warn troops along the wall of an approaching enemy.'"

Scary.

And smelly.

Worse, the enemy came through anyway. The wall is not continuous, Katie said, but built in segments, and invaders were able to go around the different parts of the wall.

"The final sections were completed in the 1500s during the Ming dynasty," Calvin added.

"Wow, that's a 1,700-year construction project," my mom said.

"More than one million people died building this tourist attraction," Katie said.

"AlvinAlvin," Bean Sprout sang. "You're standing on the world's longest cemetery."

I froze.

I didn't need to know that.

I have coimetrophobia. I'm allergic to cemeteries. I needed to get out of there fast!

Lucky for me, I had seen a sign for a quick exit.

I ran in that direction and found:

An Open Letter to Visitors

Toboggan-run is an adventure sport.
Please observe the following rules:

1. People with heart disease, hypertension, lumbar, mental disease, drunk and pregnant is not allowed.

2. Sick and elderly and children who is less than 1.3 metre in height or under 10 years old must be accompanied by an adult.

3. When sliding, please keep a safe distance. In case of collision, the rear passenger will be held legally full responsibility.

4. To avoid the sliding toboggan turn over in the corners, please the body lean to the center to overcome the centrifugal force and not allowed to stop to take pictures when sliding.

5. For your own safety, please observe the above rules, or you can take the cable car down!

Sincerely,
Beijing Mutianyu Great Wall Speed Chute Amusement Co., Ltd.

"We're not leaving yet, are we?" Katie asked. "Usually we climb to the top of the watchtower. We can't leave without doing that."

"Wait, we can't go yet!" my mom cried. "I haven't taken any pictures."

But it was too late.

I climbed in, and my dad had to jump in right after me on account of Rule No. 2. And once my dad and I were on our way down, everyone else hopped onto the ride too. We all had to stay together and not get separated.

And when you take the speed chute, it's over, just like that.

No swinging from a dangerous cable.

No life flashing before your eyes.

Nothing but extreme g-forces in tight turns at face-peeling speeds.

If you're lucky.

But if you were behind me and my dad, you got even luckier. You got the scenic ride. That meant you had time to enjoy the view. You could see the mountains in the distance. You could see the grass poking through the snow.

You could watch the sun setting, very slowly, over the trees.

I had my hand on the brake *all* the way down.

"C'mon, Alvin, let's go!" Calvin cried.

"Don't be such a slowpoke!" Katie shouted.

"AlvinAlvinyougottaletgoofthebrake!" Bean Sprout screamed.

"ALVINHOTHISISN'TAKIDDIE RIDE!" Anibelly shrieked.

"*Waaaaaaaaaaaaaaaaaaaaaah!*" cried the trout, who was strapped to my dad, who couldn't nurse her.

"*Kuaide! Kuaide!*" shouted the Chinese tourists.

It was very loud and noisy on the chute. Like a party!

The only one not making any noise was my mom. I think she was pretty steamed about not getting any pictures.

And my dad didn't get to make a speech about his bucket list. But he sure was swearing up a Shakespearean storm. "What manner of travel is this when thou hath thy paws on thy brakes???!!!" he screamed.

Nobody got any souvenirs. (You can't shop when all the stands at the bottom are closed by the time you get there.)

But TGFOCAD. Thank God For Our Car And Driver, who was ready and waiting for us to make a quick getaway, just like in the movies.

CHAPTER SIX

Indoor Vacation

the next day I was looking forward to seeing the Forbidden City on account of I never did see much of the Great Wall. When you're traveling it's important to see some historical stuff and to buy some souvenir candy; otherwise what's the point of leaving home for so long and wearing all your clothes all at once and pulling around an empty suitcase?

The Forbidden City was the palace and home of Chinese emperors for almost six hundred years. It's surrounded by a high wall and moats and bridges to keep out aliens and ordinary people, which gave me an idea for all the holes that I dig in my yard. I could connect all the holes to make a moat to keep out *girls*.

But the Air Quality Index was still too high to go out without breathing to death. So today was an indoor vacation day, just like indoor recess at school when the weather is scary.

Hooray!!! I love the great indoors.

First, Bean Sprout said we needed to take a closer look at the Christmas tree in the lobby. It was a great idea! I love Christmas trees!

But my dad said the Christmas tree in their living room was enough for him. He wasn't about to go up and down thirty-two flights just to see a tree.

Bah! Humbug!

"It's actually only twenty-eight flights," Katie said. "Floors four, thirteen, fourteen and twenty-four are missing due to the fact that four is a bad-luck number in China, and thirteen is gone too, just in case."

Wow! Four fewer floors! It was good news to me!

Calvin raced me down the stairs while the girls took the elevator, and the grown-ups stayed in the living room on the thirty-second/twenty-eighth floor, drinking tea.

Downstairs, the tree was really beautiful.

Other kids were standing around it too.

"We helped decorate it," Bean Sprout said proudly.

"We put up the angels," Katie said. "Each of the angels holds a Christmas wish from an orphan. You can take an angel, get the gift and put it in the donation box. When Christmas comes, we'll deliver them to the children."

"Like Santa Claus!" Anibelly cried.

"Like elves!" Katie said.

"Like Buddhist monks!" Bean Sprout squealed.

I took an angel down. It looked Chinese. It was holding Chinese characters. I flipped it over. On the back was the word "friend."

"This child wants a friend for Christmas," Katie said.

"What does this one say?" Anibelly asked, grabbing an angel.

Calvin turned it over.

"'Shoes, size thirty-two,'" Calvin read.

"And this one wants a book," Katie said, pointing to another. She didn't have to flip it over. Katie could read Chinese!

"I'm glad you have Christmas in China," Calvin said. "I thought I was going to miss it."

"It's not everywhere in China," Katie said. "It's only where foreign people live. To the Chinese, it's a strange holiday about skinny guys wearing red suits that are too big, and putting up trees and lights in strange places, and using extra electricity."

I blinked. I stared at the angel in my hand. "Friend"? How do you give a friend for Christmas? Do you wrap someone up? Would they fit in the donation box? Why didn't this person just write "candy"? Or "dump truck"? Or "electric train set"?

"Do we get whatever it says on the angel and put it in the box?" Anibelly asked. "Then we surprise them on Christmas Day?"

"Yup," Katie said. "That's the idea."

"What if someone doesn't get their wish?" I asked.

"It's okay," Katie said. "You don't always get your wish. But hopefully, there'll be enough presents to go around."

"What if we don't want to get the thing it says?" I asked.

"Then put it back on the tree," Bean Sprout said. "And pick another."

So I put it back on the tree.

As soon as I did, the angel spun and turned itself around so that "friend" was staring at me again.

It was not a good sign.

It was creepy!

I didn't pick another.

I turned and sprinted up the stairs, all thirty-two or twenty-eight flights, whatever it was.

•●•●•

"Look!" Anibelly said as soon as we all got back to the apartment. She ran to show her angel to my mom. "I'm going to buy shoes for an orphan!"

"And I'm buying a book!" Calvin said, waving his angel.

"Katie couldn't wait to show you her community service project," Uncle Jonathan said. "She's put a lot of work into it."

"She contacted an orphanage and helped the

children make the ornaments," Aiyi said. "Then both girls passed out flyers in our building to let everyone know."

"What a great idea," my mom said. "It's very thoughtful."

"Yup," said Bean Sprout. "Katie is very thoughtful."

Katie beamed.

Then my dad turned to me. "What does *your* angel say?"

Silence.

"He put his angel back on the tree!" Anibelly said.

"And he didn't take another one," Bean Sprout added.

Silence.

My dad was not impressed.

He looked shocked.

Maybe I had broken one of the rules of being a gentleman. I wasn't sure. I couldn't remember. But once you've seen what my dad looks like when I forget the rules, you never forget. And he looked like that.

CHAPTER SEVEN

The Passport Game

i turned and ran into our bedroom, and I stood next to the air-purifying machine. No more scary orphan ornaments. No scary dad face. It was the safest place to be.

But not for long.

The gang hurried in after me.

"AlvinAlvin," Bean Sprout said. "Let's play travel. You guys are tourists and I'm your tour guide."

"We already played that yesterday," Katie said. "Besides, that's only fun when you're at the actual sites."

"It's fun at home too," Bean Sprout said, waving her little flag. "It's fun everywhere."

"We can play a different version of travel," Katie said. "You guys are the tourists, and Calvin and I will be passport control."

"What's that?" Anibelly asked.

"Those are the people who stamp your passports when you come into a country and when you leave," Katie said.

"The rules of the game are right here in my book," Calvin said, flipping quickly to a page.

"'A valid passport and visa are needed to enter China,'" Calvin read. "'Passports must be presented when checking into hotels and when purchasing air, train or bus tickets for travel within the country. Travelers are advised to keep their passports in a safe place. In the case of a lost or stolen passport, travelers must immediately contact their own embassy or consulate to report the loss and to obtain a replacement. Getting a replacement can be a major hassle. Expect delays.'"

It sounded fun!

The big sofa bed, where my parents slept, was the Beijing airport.

The bass-in-net, where the minnow slept, which had high walls, was the Forbidden City. The rug next to it was Tiananmen Square.

The window seat was Chengdu, home of the panda breeding place, where you can snuggle with baby pandas and learn all about them. They're so cute!

The coffee table was Zhucheng, home of the world's largest dinosaur pit, where you can see bones sticking up all over the place!

Anibelly's little bed was Shaolin Temple, birthplace of kung fu.

Calvin's top bunk was Tiger Leaping Gorge, one of the deepest gorges in the world, with a wild rushing river at the bottom that will suck you away if you fall.

And my bottom bunk was the Lantian Man site.

"What's the Lantian Man site?" I asked.

"Some of the first people in the history of the world lived there," Katie said.

"Oh."

Normally, I like old people. But this was not normal. This was China, where people were inventing stuff as soon as the earth began cooling, which gave me a bad, sinking feeling that these dudes were fossils.

"No thanks," I said. "It's too old and creepy."

"How 'bout the Peking Man site, then?" Katie asked. "That's not as old."

But he still sounded dead. I shook my head.

"Fine, you can be the China Art Museum in Shanghai," Katie said. "There's a lot of new stuff there. Modern art. Instead of looking at the past, you can look at the future of China."

Katie's not bad, for a girl.

In fact, she's kind of impressive.

So I wanted to impress her too.

"I like art," I peeped.

Katie smiled.

"I like *modern* art," I tried again.

Katie was unimpressed.

So I let her have it.

"I know where our passports are!" I said.

I turned and ran into the closet. I had seen where my dad put our passports for safekeeping. They were in his fanny pack that he wears when he travels. It doesn't sit on his fanny. It hangs below his belly, which is like stringing a hammock under a cliff.

Wearing a fanny pack is no way to impress a girl. It looks terrible. So I didn't wear it. I only reached in and took out our passports so we could play the passport game.

Then I stopped.

I looked at my dad's passport. It has a million stamps in it, not like mine, which has only one.

I flipped through the pages.

I looked at all his stamps. Myanmar. Laos. Thailand. Vietnam. Cambodia. Malaysia. Indonesia. Micronesia. Polynesia. Rapa Nui. Chile. Peru. Argentina. Senegal. Mauritania. Kenya. Greece. Turkey. And my favorite—a penguin stamp from Port Lockroy, Antarctica. It's fantastic!

My dad's a super-duper traveler. He knows how to catch planes, trains, chicken buses, tuk-tuks, funiculars, gondolas and cable cars. He's traveled by camel, elephant and water buffalo. He's gone fishing with one foot in Asia and the other foot in Europe. He's seen the aurora borealis and the *Mona Lisa.* He's been on safari. He's worn a sampot. He's seen the Pope and waved at the Queen.

Katie would be really impressed.

I came *this* close to using my dad's passport for our passport game.

But I didn't.

I knew better.

If you get caught using someone else's passport, Calvin told me, you could get booted from China.

That's the good news.

The bad news was that if my dad caught me playing with his passport—even though it was only a game—I could get booted from life.

"AlvinAlvin!" I heard Bean Sprout shout from the next room. "What's taking you so long?"

"C'mon, Alvin," Anibelly said. "Let's play!"

So I hurried out of the closet with only my own passport and Anibelly's, and into our game. Calvin didn't need his, on account of he and Katie were passport control.

How to play Passport to China.

① Divide your group into tourists and officials.

② Turn some furniture into tourist attractions.

③ Turn beds into airports, train stations and museums.

④ Tourists must show their passports.

⑤ Officials must stamp the passports.

⑥ Pet a panda!

⑦ Take a hike!

⑧ Learn some Kung fu!

⑨ Look at art!

⑩ Stand by the air-purifying machine!

⑪ Game continues until the carp wakes up and cries.

Oops! We forgot she was in the room!

CHAPTER EIGHT

How to Be a Chinese Tourist

after we had already visited all of China without leaving our room, I didn't see the point of going *out* to do it again the next day, especially since my dad's knees were crying all the way down the stairs, and crying all the way up again when I realized I'd forgotten my PDK, which needed supplies.

Worse, going out meant walking past the Christmas tree where the "friend" ornament was shouting at me all the way from across the lobby, and I was afraid my dad would hear it too, but he didn't. Like I said, my dad's as old as dirt, and when you're that old, you're going to miss a few things.

It was especially silly to go out when it was still so gray it looked like rain, but not dark like a total eclipse, as it had been the day before. Aiyi said the sun never comes out in Beijing anymore, and the skies wouldn't get any clearer than this, so off we went to see some sights.

When our car stopped and we jumped out, Pan drove away again, just as he had at the Great-Wall-that-wasn't-a-wall, to park somewhere and wait for us. He's so lucky.

"Welcome to Tiananmen Square, everyone!" Bean Sprout shouted in my ear.

We were standing in the middle of a HUGE flat, treeless place. It looked nothing like the Tiananmen Square in our room yesterday. Instead, this was so big—gasp!—it was the perfect

place for aliens to land a UFO and kidnap tourists for human experiments! There were tourists everywhere—in ugly hats—being led around like pigs on their way to becoming pork chops, by tour guides waving little flags.

"Ten-an-men," Calvin said, reading from his book. "It means 'Heavenly Peace Gate.'"

"The square is named for the main gate to the Forbidden City over there," Katie said, pointing to a large red building. "This is one of the largest city squares in the world."

"And that's the Mütter Museum," Bean Sprout said in a low whisper, pointing to a building across the way. She pulled her cap lower and shuddered.

"You mean the mummy mausoleum," Katie corrected her. "That's where they keep Mao Zedong's mummied body. He was the leader of the Community Party. The Chinese line up at six in the morning to see it."

"He must have thrown some party," Calvin said.

But line up to see a *dead* body?

No way!!!

Lucky for me, Bean Sprout was freaked out too, and her little flag moved quickly in the opposite direction. "This way to the Forbidden City!" she said.

Boy, was I glad to be heading toward the Heavenly Peace Gate and not the mummy museum, which sounded a lot like certain places in Concord where dead authors are still giving tours.

But the closer we got to the gate, the less heavenly and less peaceful it looked. Large crowds were posing for pictures in front of a HUGE picture of a man hanging from the center of the red building. His eyes followed everyone, everywhere.

"That's him," Bean Sprout hissed, pointing to the portrait. "That's the mummy."

I stopped dead in my tracks.

Ooomph!

I bit the dust.

Birds twittered.

Stars spun.

Then little hands peeled me off the ground. It was Bean Sprout and Anibelly.

"AlvinAlvin," one of them sang. "Yougottakeepmovingorthey'llmowyourightover."

"Lalalalalala," sang the other. "Lalalalalalala."

Oooh. They really fried my dumpling.

Normally, stopping dead in my tracks in Concord, Massachusetts, which is hard to spell, and where there are also lots of tourists, is no problem. But stopping dead in my tracks in front of the Go-to-Heaven-and-Rest-in-Peace Gate was the wrong thing to do.

So right there and then I learned the rules.

HOW TO BE A CHINESE TOURIST

1. Wear an ugly hat.
2. Keep your eye on a little flag.
3. Keep moving.
4. Keep moving.
5. Just keep moving!!!

And if you're a gentleman, you also have to strap your baby on your chest as a human shield and stand in line for tickets, which my dad was doing with Uncle Jonathan while the rest of us floated in the waves of tourists pushing to get inside.

"'Only the emperor, his family, servants and invited dignitaries were allowed inside,'" Calvin read from his book.

"It was forbidden for the common people to enter," Katie added. "If you or I went in, we'd be executed on the spot."

Executed on the spot???!!!!

"AAAAAAAAAAAARRRRRRRRGG!!!"

It sounded like an execution!

I turned.

I saw my dad.

Two orange caps were bobbing and spinning near the ticket booths— My dad and Uncle Jonathan were searching for something on the ground.

Bean Sprout was right—our bright orange caps were easy to spot. They stood out from all the groups of boring-colored caps. Up and down, and round and round the orange caps went. Finally, they stopped and headed our way.

My dad did not look well.

He looked like he'd been in a fight with an egg beater—and lost.

"Honey," he said to my mom. "My passport's gone."

My mom gasped.

"Gone?" she said. "Are you sure?"

My dad pawed through his fanny pack.

"It's not here," he said.

"We looked all over," Uncle Jonathan said. "Maybe it fell out and someone snatched it. Foreign passports are worth a lot, especially a US passport of a Chinese-looking guy."

"What are we going to do?" my mom asked.

"Well, there's no point in ruining everyone's day," Uncle Jonathan said. "Here are the tickets. You guys take the kids and enjoy the Forbidden City. Pan will wait for you."

"We're going back to their apartment to search," my dad said. "If my passport's not there, I'm heading over to the embassy."

My poor dad.

Yesterday he missed the Great Wall.

Today he was going to miss everything else.

Unless I said something.

I wanted to say it.

I really did.

I had the words in my mouth. . . .

I even lined them up. . . .

And got them ready. . . . "I saw your passport yesterday" was what I wanted to say.

But I said nothing.

If I said that, I would have to say *what* I did with it.

And the problem with that was I wasn't supposed to take out his passport. Worse, I had no idea what I'd done with it.

None.

One peep and I was dead meat!

Then my dad unstrapped the sleeping cod from his chest and strapped her onto my mom.

That's the problem with dudes. They can't nurse a baby. I know. I've tried. And babies get hungry sooner or later, so this meant that he was expecting to be gone for a long time.

"Take care of your mother," my dad said to me and Calvin.

It sounded like he wasn't expecting to be back.

At all.

Gulp.

Then he and Uncle Jonathan were gone, just like that.

CHAPTER NINE

Dragons, Dragons, Everywhere

the problem with not confessing your crimes is everything.

First, there are the gigan-
tic red doors built to keep out
giants, aliens and people who
don't confess their crimes.
Red means stop. Red means
forbidden.

Red is the color of blood
when you're executed on the spot for coming
into the Forbidden City.

Second, if you get past the doors and manage to escape execution, then you run into a pair of sharp-toothed, sharp-clawed lions at the first bridge and moat. Anyone can see that it is *not* a welcome sign. It's a fancy No Trespassing sign. Their sharp eyes followed me.

"Smile!" my mom said, holding up her phone.

Everyone smiled in front of the lions. Everyone, that is, except me. I had hurried past the lions and was on my way up the stairs. . . .

But 9,999 dragons await you along the stairs that you have to climb to reach the first building! They are breathing fire and baring their talons.

The Forbidden City is full of dragons.

They hiss and snarl from every wall, corner, bridge, ceiling and rooftop.

They are the guard dogs.

And the gargoyles.

They coil around the columns.

They watch you from everywhere.

Lucky for me, there were LOTS of tourists for the dragons to watch.

But unlucky for me, there were LOTS of tourists shoving and pushing and shouting all over the place.

Worse, they were pushing and shoving *me*!

Phatttttt! I was fly-flattened against the side of the first huge building, just like that.

My guts pushed out.

My eyeballs popped.

I looked through the see-through plastic barrier.

Yikes! More dragons! They were crawling all over the place! Dragons lunged from the old carpets. They coiled themselves around the tables and chairs. They danced on the ceiling.

"'This is the Hall of Supreme Harmony. It is the largest wooden building in China,'" I heard Calvin reading from somewhere behind me. "'Nearly the size of an American football field, it is the most important and grandest building in the Forbidden City.'"

The noisy crowd pressed in.

"Look, that's the Dragon Throne," Katie said. "The emperor ruled China from there. This is where official ceremonies and meetings took place."

"If we had lived one hundred years ago, we never could have seen this with our own eyes," my mom added, "let alone stood so close to it."

I saw it with my own eyes, all right. Dragons coiled from the arms and back of a HUGE, ENORMOUS chair. More dragons leaped and leered from the screen behind it.

"Aaaaaaalviiiiiiin," the dragons hissed.

"Wherrrrrrre's your dad's passssssssssssport?"

Gasp!

How did they know?

Smoke puffed from their nostrils.

Fire dripped from their teeth.

Tails thrashed their scaly horrors.

The crowd pressed in, *hard*.

I slipped out, *fast*.

I hurried up some steps and over another bridge, and headed toward a huge black pot with two shiny gold dragons as handles.

"That's a fire extinguisher," Katie said, following me. "In the old days it was filled with water, and buckets were used to put out the flames."

Fire extinguishers were everywhere.

I hurried across more moats and bridges, and before I knew it—straight into another crowd as thick as books on a shelf, outside another large building.

Phuuuuuut! I was a human pancake against the wall again.

"My map says this is the Hall of Heavenly Purity," Aiyi said. "It's the largest building in the Inner Court, which was the emperor's residence."

"'The emperor slept here,'" Calvin read. "'There are two levels divided into nine rooms with twenty-seven beds. Each night the emperor would randomly choose a bed to sleep in to avoid being assassinated in his sleep.'"

Gulp.

I should have a plan like that.

"We're going too fast," Katie said. "I can't believe we're already in the Inner Court."

Too fast? We weren't going fast enough!

"We went too fast at the Great Wall, and now we're going too fast at the Forbidden City!" she wailed. "We missed the official wedding chamber where the emperors got married."

"Wedding chamber? Who wants to see that?"

"I do," Katie said.

"Me too," said Bean Sprout.

"Me three," said Anibelly.

"Actually, I'd like to see that too," my mom said.

Oh brother.

I needed to do something *fast*, or we were going to start all over again in the Forbidden City, where the dragons knew me by name, which made me feel so sick, I slipped off the wall.

"What's the matter with AlvinAlvin?" Bean Sprout asked.

"I think he needs the bathroom," Anibelly said.

"Oh, Alvin," my mom said. "We just got started."

But my mom knows that when you gotta go, you gotta go.

The good news was that everyone headed into the gift shop to wait while my mom and the haddock on her chest took me to the men's room. No one headed back to the beginning of the tour. Whew!

The bad news was that the bathroom wasn't what I expected.

I looked in one stall.

Then I looked in another.

Going to the bathroom is usually no problem. When in doubt, my dad likes to say, go to the bathroom. It's a quiet place to think and make plans.

But this was *not* a quiet place for thinking or making plans.

This was a *pit* toilet.

I'm allergic to pit toilets.

Especially ones that flush.

In fact, this was the first time I'd seen a flushing pit.

My head hung over it like a moon over an oversized dog dish.

It was a *long* way down.

What if I missed?

Or slipped?

I could fall in.

I could get flushed.

And what are the ridges on the sides for? Are you supposed to scrape the dirt off your shoes while you do your business?

I tried it. I scraped my shoes like a regular Chinese dude.

When you're in a foreign country, it's important to do what the regular people do. You should try to blend in. You should observe how they do things and try it yourself. You should follow their rules. You should learn their language. If you're allergic to their toilets, you can at least do half of it right—and clean your shoes.

Then you should get your mom to take you into the ladies' room. It's always nicer over there anyway.

"Are you feeling better?" my mom asked when I came out of the men's room. She looked worried. "You were in there for a very long time."

I looked at my shoes.

"Can you take me to the ladies' room now?" I asked.

"What?" My mom looked at me. "You've been acting very strange."

She felt my forehead. "No fever," she said.

But my mom knows you don't need a fever to be sick. And when I'm sick, a ladies' room is the best place to keep an eye on me, just in case.

So we got in line. (There's always a line to use the nicer restroom.)

Then we went in. The three of us squeezed into one stall.

What???!!!

This was no ladies' room.

This was another pit toilet!!!

With the same powerful sucking action!

My mom said I only needed a lesson in how to use it.

"Just squat," she said.

Then my mom was tugging and pulling me over it, and I was tugging and pulling back. If I had known this was going to happen, I would have stayed in the men's room!

Well, this explained a lot of things . . . such as how they made eunuchs back in the old days. If you don't know what a eunuch is, I'm not going to tell you. Calvin said tens of thousands of them used to work in the Forbidden City. And they were not happy dudes, you can count on that.

"IAMNOTUSINGAFLUSHINGPITTOILETAREYOUCRAZY???!!!"

I screamed at the top of my lungs.

And if you think that it was a silent scream on account of I was all freaked out by the pit toilets, you'd be wrong. It was the loudest scream in the Forbidden City in the history of China ever, next to the eunuchs'.

CHAPTER TEN

Peeking Duck

no one said anything about starting over in the Forbidden City after that. We were back in the car before I knew it, and everyone had a special souvenir from the gift shop but me.

Anibelly carried a new coin purse.

Bean Sprout had bought a little fan with—yikes!—a dragon on it.

Katie wore a small jade good-luck charm.

Aiyi had a scarf for my mom. It was very pretty. It made her look better after spending the morning in the toilet with me.

But all I had was a sore throat.

Worse, my PDK was still empty.

"You should have a T-shirt that says 'All I Saw in the Forbidden City Was the Toilet,'" Calvin said. He was wearing a new T-shirt that said "I Climbed the Great Wall."

"Well, you didn't climb the Great Wall," I said.

"I didn't see much of the Forbidden City either, thanks to you," Calvin said. "But I really wanted this shirt anyway."

"It looks good," I said.

"Thanks," said Calvin.

I was glad I had a good word for Calvin. Usually, I don't have any good words for him on account of he's always kicking my butt and not letting me touch his things. But he hasn't kicked my butt since we left home. He's been reading his book instead, and looking like he's on a field trip. "You're a good tourist," I added. I could hardly believe that I had a *second* good word for him! It was not normal.

And Calvin knew it.

Oops.

Calvin gave me the eye.

Then he gave me the other eye.

I hate it when he does that.

Calvin can read my mind. It's one of his talents.

And the problem with that was that I was thinking about you-know-what-I-didn't-tell-my-dad.

"What did you do?" Calvin asked.

"Nothing," I said.

"Why do you look so guilty, then?" he asked.

All eyes turned to me.

Gulp.

"AlvinAlvin!" Bean Sprout burst into song. *"You better watch out, you better not cry, better not pout, I'm telling you why. Santa Claus is coming to town!"*

"*He sees you when you're sleeping,*" Anibelly chimed in. "*He knows when you're awake.*"

"*He knows if you've been bad or good,*" they both sang, "*so be good for goodness' sake!*"

Ugggggggh. It's the creepiest Christmas song ever!

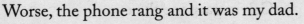

Worse, the phone rang and it was my dad.

"Are you sure?" my mom said.

"CrackCrackCrackSsssSsssSss," said my dad.

My mom looked worried.

"SsssSssssSsssClakClakClak," my dad said.

My mom looked worrieder.

Then she hung up.

It was not good news.

There was no passport at the apartment. So my dad and Uncle Jonathan were heading to the embassy.

No passport? Did they check the closet? Maybe I had dropped it in the back of the closet when . . .

I felt sick again.

Very, very sick.

"Mom," Anibelly said. "Alvin doesn't look so good!"

"Oh, darling," my mom said. "When your dad's not having a good day, you don't have one either, do you?"

I shook my head.

"We should get some lunch in you," Aiyi said. "You'll feel much better after lunch."

Then she said some Chinese words to Pan, and soon our minivan stopped and everyone jumped out, even Pan. He did not drive off. Instead, he walked into the restaurant with us. Aiyi had invited him to join us for lunch.

"It's important to feed and take care of the people who help you," Aiyi said. "Pan either eats with us, or if there's a bunch of drivers around, like there was at the Great Wall, he'll prefer to sit at the drivers' table."

Calvin and I sat up as straight as chopsticks.

Being a Chinese driver sounded better and better!

"We're very lucky to have good help," Aiyi said. "They give up being with their own families to be with ours."

My mom nodded. She knows what it's like to have good help too, on account of she has me and Calvin. We're gentlemen. We like to do all the work. And soon we'll be able to drive her around!

"Speaking of help," Aiyi continued, "when you have laundry, just set it out on a chair and our maid will take care of it for you."

"Thank you," my mom said. "That would be great."

Then our lunch came out.

Peeking duck. It's a Beijing specialty. A special duck chef comes to your table to put on a show for you. After that, you put stuff on a pancake, roll it up and eat it. But if you can't wait for the show, you can eat Peeking duck anyway.

HOW TO EAT PEEKING DUCK

1. Take a pancake.
2. Dip your chopstick in the duck sauce.
3. Draw a duck on your pancake peeking at you.
4. Draw your name next to your duck.
5. Eat!

It was very yummy! Aiyi had ordered many other dishes too. Tofu. Dumplings. Soup. Fish. Shrimp. Noodles. Greens. Rolls. Rice. Everything!

It looked super-duper!

It smelled super-duper!

I could have eaten all of it, just like that! I was so hungry!!!

Lucky for me, I didn't.

I caught myself just in the nick of time.

When you're in China, you don't just dig in. You have to use your chopsticks and put something on your neighbor's plate first. You wait until everyone has something. Then you eat.

Aiyi served my mom and Pan first. Then she poured us tea.

How to say Thank You when Someone Pours You Tea

① Put the three middle fingers of your right hand together.

② Bend them over so that they're facing the ground.

③ Tap the table three times with your fingertips next to your cup.
(It looks like kowtowing, a deep bending over at the waist, which is the Chinese way of saying you're important, I appreciate you!)

I already knew this on account of that's how we do it in Concord too. My gunggung and pohpoh taught me.

The other thing I knew was not to let your neighbor's teacup get empty. When someone has sipped their tea, pour more for them!

So I did.

I filled Katie's cup. She was mad at me earlier,

but it's hard to stay mad at someone who pours you tea.

Then I filled my mom's cup. She smiled and tapped the table, which gave me the idea that pouring my dad some tea later might be a good way to soften the blow coming to me. It might even work better than crying.

"I'm glad you're feeling better," my mom said.

The more tea I poured, the better I felt!

I felt good enough even to fill Calvin's cup, which normally I wouldn't do.

Calvin tapped the table.

He was suspicious of me earlier, and he was still suspicious of me now. I could see it in his eyes. He was watching me very carefully.

Gulp.

Making people smile in China is easy. All you need is a pot of tea. But getting your brother to stop reading your mind is not so easy.

And the problem with that was I forgot to stop pouring his tea. I was too busy watching him watch me.

"Whoaaaaa!" Calvin cried. "Whoaaaaaaaaa!"

He jumped away from the table, which should have been the end of that. But Calvin likes to tuck the tablecloth into his shirt like a napkin so that he doesn't get crumbs in his lap. So the tablecloth set sail with him. SWOOOOOSH!

Just then a man wearing a white surgical mask rolled a little cart up to our table. I think he was the special chef that Aiyi had told us about. On his cart was a dead duck.

"*Eeeeeeeeeeeeeeeek!*" Anibelly shrieked.

"Aaaaaaaaaaaaaack!" Bean Sprout screamed.

CLANGCLANGCLANGCLANG!!!

CLINKCLINKCLINKCLINK!!!!

CRRRAAAAASH!

"Waaaaaaaaaaaaaaaaaaaaaaah!!!" the flounder cried.

I dropped my teapot.

CLUNK!

THUDTHUDTHUDTHUDTHUD!!!

Everything happened all at once. And I screamed, "A *real* duck? With eyes? And a heart that beats? I thought we were only eating our duck paintings!!!"

I had been doing so well with my Chinese manners, but I wasn't doing so well anymore.

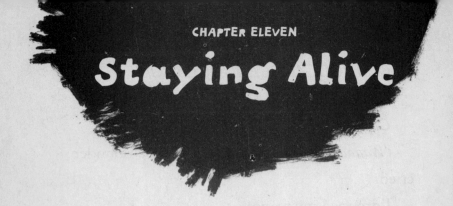

CHAPTER ELEVEN

Staying Alive

if you think that I was having a horrible vacation, wait till you hear what happened next.

For the first time in my life, I rode the elevator. All the way up to the thirty-second-floor-minus-four-bad-luck-floors, and I dashed into the closet before anyone could see where I was going. I had to find my dad's passport, fast!

But when I got to the closet, it was very clean and tidy, not like it was the night before, when I'd left everything in a heap on the floor. It was very strange.

"Whence goeth mine bawbling, flea-infested, fusty trimmings?" I said.

I turned around.

I froze.

There on my bed, where the China Art Museum used to be, was a stack of all my clothes, pressed and folded. Like new. I've never seen my clothes look so nice!

Did the maid do my laundry???!!!

What happened to my dad's passport???

I tore through my clothes.

T-shirts!

Pants!

Socks!

Underwear!

I unzipped zippers.

I undid buttons.

I ripped through Velcro.

Nothing.

Then something. Fell. Out.

From one of my pukiest pantaloon pockets, out came—ZOUNDS!—a little blue ball.

Oops.

This was *not* what I was looking for.

What am I going to do with this???!!!

Oh, I was going to be SOOOO busted.

Quickly, I stuffed the ball into a different pocket.

Then I ran out to the living room, where everyone was listening to my dad tell about *his* horrible day.

"We were in line for five hours," my dad said, "before I found out I needed a police report that said I'd lost my passport."

"And he needed new color passport photos too," Uncle Jonathan added.

"And a copy of my old passport," my dad said. "I didn't have any of that."

"What are you going to do?" my mom asked.

"I'll have to try again tomorrow," my dad sighed.

"Look on the bright side," my mom said. "Losing your passport is better than losing one of our kids somewhere."

All the grown-ups nodded and chuckled.

"Most days, I would agree," my dad said, giving me a strong pat on the back. "Right, son?"

Gulp.

I didn't know what to say.

I blinked.

I ran back into our room.

I turned out the light.

I slipped under the covers.

And closed my eyes.

We had just gotten back from dinner and

it wasn't quite bedtime yet, but it was bedtime for me.

Usually, I'm the last one to go to sleep on account of I need to keep an eye on things. But not tonight. The day had gone from bad to worse. So I had to end the day before it ended me.

In the dark, I listened to the windy breath of the air-purifying machine.

I heard the voices of my family coming from the living room.

Everyone was still visiting and having a good time.

My dad was now making jokes about his wasted day.

My mom was laughing about our tug-of-war in the ladies' room.

Calvin was reading something from his book. (Probably to Katie.)

And I could hear Anibelly and Bean Sprout singing another Christmas carol. *"Deck the Wall with boughs of rice cakes, fa-la-la-la-la-la-la-la-la!"*

That's the thing about my family. They could have a really rotten day, and the next thing you know, they're laughing about it and rolling up rice balls in seaweed and dipping stuff in soy sauce and listening to classical music like Madonna.

Not me.

A tear leaked out of my eye.

I blinked.

Then another tear leaked out of my other eye.

I blinked at the dark sky outside my window, but nothing blinked back. No moon. No stars. Nothing.

Nothing in China is like anything in Concord.

The lines are long.

The toilets are deadly.

Everything is HUGE, like it's built for giants.

Even Christmas doesn't feel like Christmas.

The Santas are skinny.

The ornaments are scary.

Worse, I put someone's wish back on the tree.

Gulp.

More tears fell out of my eyes.

I was having the worst vacation of my life.

"Waaaaaaaaaaaaaaaaaaaaaaaaaaaaaaah!" I cried.

Then I turned over and cried myself to sleep.

CHAPTER TWELVE

A Chopstickful of Chinese Medicine

when you're traveling overseas and things don't go as planned, you should have a Plan B, my dad says. My dad is really organized. He has a plan for everything.

His Plan B was to go back to the embassy.

And my mom and Aiyi's plan was to take everyone shopping. No more sightseeing until the "guys can join us," they said.

But what happens when your Plan B still doesn't go as planned?

I had stomach cramps and needed to use the bathroom in a bad way.

"There's a Chinese medicine clinic not too far from here," Aiyi said. "They'll have just the cure for that."

So my dad needed a Plan B to his Plan B, which was to take me to the doctor.

My mom bundled me up. And my dad carried me down twenty-eight flights of stairs, on account of an elevator is still an elevator when you're sick, and into a waiting cab.

HOW TO TAKE A TAXI IN CHINA

1. Give the driver a piece of paper with your destination written in Chinese.
2. Cuddle close with your dad.
3. Cuddle closer.
4. Just cuddle.

I love being with my dad.

"The last thing you want to do overseas is get

arrested," my dad said, putting his arm around me in the warm cab. "That's the first rule of traveling abroad. Obey the laws of the country you're in. Follow their rules. Respect their customs. Don't get arrested."

I nodded.

I love listening to my dad. He has a lot to say. He knows a lot about getting along with people and staying out of trouble. And he's full of good advice.

"And the second rule is, don't get sick," my dad said. "Medical treatments differ wherever you go. Sometimes the remedy is worse than the disease. You never know. It's best to avoid it if you can."

But sometimes you can't.

And that's when you end up at the Chinese medicine clinic.

The doctor was in.

She was sitting at a desk talking to a patient. Other patients were standing around and leaning close to hear what the doctor had to say. As soon as we walked in, the doctor stopped.

"How old is he?" she asked my dad.

"Seven and a half," my dad said.

The doctor said something in Chinese to the patient at her desk. The patient got up, and the doctor waved to my dad to sit down with me in his lap. It was my turn, just like that!

"Children first." The doctor winked at me.

My dad explained that my tummy was sick.

"Diarrhea?" the doctor asked.

Everyone leaned in closer.

How embarrassing! I had to tell the doctor about my troubles in front of everyone.

"How many times?" the doctor asked.

I wanted to disappear!

No one moved. No one even breathed, until I held up ten fingers—and flashed them.

Then everyone was talking all at once. It sounded like they all had something to say about how to cure you-know-what!

The doctor wrote my answers down in Chinese.

Then she took my pulse for a long, long time.

Finally, she said my pulse told her that I was scared of many things. "Be brave," she said. "Be happy. When you're scared, you will get sick." As for my tummy, she told me, "Eat only hot or warm food."

Everyone in the room nodded.

Then the doctor asked my dad a bunch of questions and took his pulse too.

"Stress," she said to my dad. "Too much vacation."

The other patients had a lot to say about that too. Going to the doctor in China is a spectator sport with audience participation!

At last, the doctor took us into the next room, where a few patients were lying on beds, resting quietly. The doctor pointed to two empty beds side by side. I lay down on one, and my dad lay down on the other.

The good news about Chinese medicine, my pohpoh and gunggung had told me, is that everything is gentle and healing to your body. For thousands of years, the Chinese have cured themselves using plants and acupuncture.

The bad news is, medicine is medicine.

And I'm generally allergic to stuff like that.

"What's acupuncture?" I asked my dad.

But before my dad could explain, he had turned into—gasp!—a human pincushion!

The doctor had stuck him with needles all over!

My poor dad!

Then the doctor turned to me.

"Relax," the doctor said. "Close your eyes."

Before I knew it, I was a human pincushion too! YIKES!!! Then the doctor told us to rest, and left the room.

"Dad?" I said. I dared not move a picometer.

"Son," my dad said. He dared not move a femtometer.

"Did you know this was going to happen to us?" I asked.

"No," my dad said. "I was not expecting this."

"Am I going to die?" I asked. Tears rolled down my cheeks.

"No," my dad said. "I think this is supposed to be good for us."

"You mean this isn't letting the air out of us?" I asked.

"No," my dad said. "We're not balloons."

"I'm scared," I said.

"I know," my dad said, reaching out to hold my hand. "The needles are supposed to move our chi."

"What's chi?" I asked.

"Energy," my dad said. "We're made up of energy. According to Chinese medicine, when our energy gets stuck, we get sick. The needles help release the stuck chi. Then we feel better."

Release what?

Oh no!

This was not good news.

"Which needle?" I asked. "I DON'T WANT MY STUFF COMING OUT AT ALL!!!"

Silence.

My dad stared at me.

I stared at the needles in the backs of my hands.

Then everything spilled out, all at once.

"Itookoutyourpassportandlostit," I said. "Thenitfelloutofmycleanlaundrybutitwasn'tyourpassportanymoreitwasalittleblueball."

My dad turned the color of bones in the desert.

He didn't breathe, not one bit.

A week went by.

Then my dad blinked.

It was all he did.

He didn't lunge for me.

He didn't scream at me.

He didn't even have a Shakespearean curse for me.

Not one.

Chinese medicine is really amazing.

Who knew that wearing quills like a porcupine would soften the blow like this?

It works better than crying!

And it sure beats being sick.

CHAPTER THIRTEEN

Fate and a Fortune-Teller

porcupuncture worked so well, my dad looked as calm as Walden Pond.

And I felt much better too. As soon as my chi got unstuck, I was healed, just like that.

"Son," my dad said as we left the crowded clinic and stepped back onto the crowded sidewalk, "I feel like a new man."

My dad breathed in deeply.

He pulled back his shoulders.

He lifted his chin.

He was a giant.

"You're not mad at me?" I asked.

"Mad at you?" my dad said. "Why should I be mad? You should be more careful, son. But it was a piece of paper. It can be replaced."

I skipped a little to keep up with my dad's long stride. We went down the street.

"The important thing is that we're healthy," my dad said. "When you have your health, you have everything. All other problems are minor."

"Really, Dad?"

"Really, son," my dad said. I love it when he calls me that. Son. I love it more than my own name. And I love it especially when he calls me that in a good mood, like he was in now.

"I'm glad you're not mad at me," I said.

My dad squeezed my hand.

"I'm glad we're together," he said, "and that we're on vacation in one of the oldest and most fascinating cultures on earth."

He was right about that.

We had walked right into the middle of a very old place.

The streets were dusty and narrow.

The houses were old and gray and close together.

A man went by with an ancient wheelbarrow.

"Where are we?" I asked my dad.

He stopped.

He turned around.

"Are we lost?" I asked.

"Not sure," my dad said. "I think we're in a hutong."

"A who?" I asked.

"'Hutong' means 'alley' or 'lane,'" my dad said. "The real culture of Beijing is in the hutongs, the city's oldest neighborhoods. Many of them have been destroyed to make room for high-rises. I really wanted to see one of these."

"How old?" I asked. Old is creepy. "Older than Concord?"

"Much older," my dad said. "Some of these were built in the 1200s when the Mongols ruled China during the Yuan dynasty. These neighborhoods formed concentric circles around the Forbidden City. Aristocrats and wealthy people lived in the spacious lanes closest to the palace, while commoners and laborers lived in the outer circles of narrower alleys."

My dad loves history and historical sites. If he could live in an old house and dress up in old-fashioned clothes and give tours, he would.

"It feels like we've stepped back in time," my dad said. His eyes filled with the gray light of the hutong. "You get a sense of what life was like for many centuries.

"The narrowest hutong is only sixteen inches wide," he continued. "When two people meet, they have to turn sideways to pass one another. And many lanes have strange names, like Skewed Tobacco Pouch Street, or Soap Street, or Nine Turns, which actually has nineteen turns."

A street with nineteen turns?

"Do you mean we're LOST, DAD???" I cried.

Then I really cried. *"Waaaaaaaaaaaaaaaah!"* Tears streamed down my face.

You'd cry too if you were lost in a crowd of more than one billion people and your dad had the vocabulary of a Chinese baby. Worse, my dad had no more pieces of paper with addresses on them. None.

"Son," my dad said, kneeling beside me and holding me firmly. "Think of this as an adventure. You're never lost on an adventure. You are always where you need to be."

"I am?"

"Sure," my dad said. "The Chinese call it destiny."

"Dusty?" I asked.

My dad shook his head. "'Fate' is another word for it. It's the belief that your life has a map. You're never lost."

I wiped my eyes on my sleeve.

"So let's just explore and enjoy this part of town together," my dad said. "After that, we'll worry about finding our way back."

Worry? I was already worried!

But my dad was not.

First we stopped for a bowl of noodles.

Then we shared a bag of sunflower seeds. You crack the shell between your teeth and you eat the middle.

After that, we stopped in a bookstore.

Then we checked out a little-pet market. I stuck my finger in the baby rabbit cages. And listened to the songbirds.

Then we watched and clapped for the yo-yo dude performing his tricks. He was super-duper!

Then we put money into an old man's can. His sign said:

#1 BEST
FORTUNE-
TELLER
CHINESE : 20 RMB
INGLISH : 40 RMB
BUY ONE, GET ONE FREE!

"A wise man you are," he said to my dad. "You are a friend and son of China from far away. You will live a long and prosperous life. You will have a long trip in China."

My dad smiled and nodded.

Then it was my turn.

"You have a smart older brother," he said, turning my face in his hand. "And two very smart younger sisters."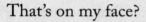

That's on my face?

"You are very loving," the fortune-teller said. "You always want to do the right thing."

That's better.

"But you don't always remember what it is."

How did he know?

Then he gave me one last glance.

"Your wife will be very pretty."

Whaaaat?

"I'MNOTGETTINGMARRIED!!!" I cried. "BESIDES, MYWIFEISGOINGTOBE AHAMSTER!!!"

After that, my dad bought a pair of stress balls—and put them in my PDK.

Then a few steps down the street, he added a yo-yo to my supplies. "Who knows," he said.

"You might have to make a living on the streets."
It was perfect!

We got ice cream.

Then we got invited to play a game of Chinese chess. I love Chinese chess! The sun was setting on a cold but not windy afternoon. Players were bundled up and bent over their games on top of plastic crates outside their homes. Everyone was pleased that I could play. My gunggung had taught me.

Finally, my dad said it was time to go.

Too bad.

"It's really super-duper here," I said.

"I had a feeling it would be," my dad said.

"Do you believe in that fortune-teller stuff?" I asked.

"Nah," my dad said. "It's just for fun."

"Maybe I would have liked living here in the old days," I said.

"Me too," my dad said.

Then, hand in hand, my dad and I headed toward the busy street where you could see tall buildings and cars and taxis zooming past and everything looked scarier than it did thousands of years ago.

CHAPTER FOURTEEN

The Ultimate Survival Gear

the fortune-teller was right.

My dad was going to be in China for a *long* time.

After he reported his missing passport to the police . . .

After he got his new photos taken . . .

After he stood in line for another entire day . . .

After all that, my dad still had to wait "up to two weeks" before returning to the embassy to pick up his new passport and visa.

Rule No. 3 for traveling overseas, my dad says, is never lose your passport, or someone else's.

The good news was that my dad was still not mad at me.

The bad news was that it messed up our itinerary. You can't buy a train or bus ticket or check into a hotel in China without your passport. Staying an extra two weeks in Beijing meant that we needed a Plan B. Our Plan A included the world's largest dinosaur pit, kung fu lessons at Shaolin Temple, and my yehyeh's village, where it floods every year and where he used to take down the doors of his house when he was a boy and paddle around for survival. Calvin was really disappointed. He wanted to do that.

Not me.

I now had to survive long enough to marry someone pretty. I'm not looking forward to it, but if that's on my dusty life map, there's nothing I can do about it but stay away from danger.

So I was in our room checking out the new stuff in my PDK when Calvin leaped out of

nowhere and chopped my head
and kicked my butt.

"Ow!" I cried. "Owwow-
owow!"

That's the problem with Calvin.
He can be a bookworm one minute and a total
Lantian dude the next.

"A fight, a fight!" Anibelly cried. "You're
busted!"

Lucky for Calvin, Bean Sprout blocked my
kung fu leg in the air and my kung fu chop in
mid-chop. Otherwise, Calvin would have suf-
fered too.

"AlvinAlvin," Bean Sprout said. "Let's go
play!"

So we did.

We followed Bean Sprout down to the lobby
(she took the stairs) to stare at the Christmas
tree (again).

The ornament that said "friend" was still
there. And it stared me smack in the eye.

"Is this all you wanted to do?" I asked.

"Yup," Bean Sprout said.

"Me too," Katie said. "Isn't it beautiful?"

"It's SOOOO beautiful," Anibelly said, wrapping her arms around me. "Isn't it, Alvin?"

I wished Anibelly wouldn't do that, but it did feel good. So I put my arm around her too.

"I'm so glad you guys are staying longer," Bean Sprout said. "It was my Christmas wish."

"Mine too," Katie said. "Having you here makes Christmas feel really special."

"It feels special to me too," Calvin said. "But Christmas is tomorrow, and most of your ornaments are still on the tree. No one's taken any."

"No worries," Katie said. "They will."

"It's the miracle of Christmas," Bean Sprout said. "You'll see."

"Yeah, you'll see!" Anibelly said. Then she and Bean Sprout did their little dance and sang "Jingle Bells." It's Anibelly's favorite.

Then Katie told us the story of the shepherds who watched their flocks by night . . .

And we all stared at the Christmas tree for seven seconds straight. Amen.

Then everyone raced for the elevators.

Everyone but me.

I'm allergic. I had to take the stairs.

But before I did, I reached for the ornament that was calling out to me.

"Friend," it said. It was a really strange wish. How do you give a person as a gift?

I put it in my PDK.

I stared at it.

It was a piece of heaven at the bottom of a dark and scary well.

How I was going to grant that wish, I had no idea. Making friends was hard. Wishing for friends was even harder.

Then I looked up.

I stood on one foot.

Then I stood on the other.

It took a long time to take *all* the angels off the tree.

And put them into my PDK.

An entire host of heavenly angels in my PDK. Who needs survival gear when you've got angels?

But how was I going to grant all those wishes?

I breathed in.

I breathed out.

Well, I didn't know that either.

All I knew was that I could hardly wait to

show my dad. I had a feeling he would help me do what I needed to do. He always does.

"Daaaaad!" I cried, dashing back up the stairs, full speed ahead. There was no time to waste. "DAAAAAAAAAAAD!"

CHAPTER FIFTEEN

You Can Make a Friend Anywhere

my dad was shocked.

But my mom was not.

"Oh, Alvin," she said, when she saw all the angel ornaments in my PDK. "What a lovely thing to do."

I nodded. Then I showed her all the money I had. I'd been saving it for a long time, not like Calvin, who spends it as soon as he gets it. I had some hung baus that my pohpoh and gunggung had given me right before our trip. And I had the money my dad had been paying me as part of our deal for me to keep quiet and be a good tourist.

"Sometimes you really surprise me," my mom said. "You are the most empathetic of my children."

I didn't like the sound of that, but I liked that my mom gave me a big, long hug and a kiss on the top of my head for being the most pathetic. I love it when she does that. I love it more than all the candy in China. Then she wiped tears from her eyes. My mom is like that. She cries whenever I do something right, and also when I do something wrong. So I gave her a hug and a kiss back.

Then my mom took me shopping.

The air was cold and gray.

The streets were crowded.

The bus was packed.

I held on to my mom with one hand and my PDK with the other.

Normally, I don't like shopping. It's not my thing.

But I do in China.

We went to a famous shopping street where nearly everything was outside and on clearance. There, my mom showed me:

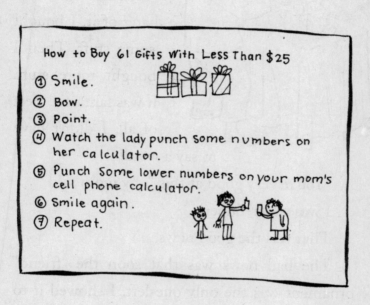

How to Buy 61 Gifts With Less Than $25

① Smile.
② Bow.
③ Point.
④ Watch the lady punch some numbers on her calculator.
⑤ Punch some lower numbers on your mom's cell phone calculator.
⑥ Smile again.
⑦ Repeat.

I watched my mom do it. You have to be very polite and patient. You have to remember your manners and not run away.

Then I tried it. It was very scary! The lady didn't punch her calculator. And I didn't get the toy that I was pointing at with my eyes.

"Eye action only works with people who know you," my mom said.

So I tried again. When I got the hang of it, I bought some stuff. Then I bought more stuff. It was fantastic! Best of all, I didn't have to say a word!

"You're very good at this," my mom said.

I was super-duper!

That was the good news.

The bad news was that soon the "friend" ornament was the only one left. I showed it to my mom.

"Well," my mom said. "You can't *buy* a friend, that's for sure. You have to *be* one."

"You mean someone's wishing for *me*?" I asked. "But I don't speak Chinese."

My mom looked at me.

I looked at all the packages in my hands.

"You don't need words to be a friend," my mom said. "You just need to be there."

Then my mom gave me some advice.

HOW TO MAKE A FRIEND ANYWHERE
1. Smile.
2. Say hello.
3. Don't run away.
4. Just don't run away.

It sounded so easy.

•.•.•

But it wasn't easy.

It was Christmas morning, and I was having a bad start. I had to get cleaned and dressed.

"Tricked!" I wailed as we set out for the orphanage. "You said I only had to *be* there. You didn't say I had to look like Calviiiiin!"

My brother Calvin is mostly neat and smells like soap. He was born that way. Not like me. I don't normally look or smell that fine. It takes hours for my mom to catch me, hold me down and scrub me off. It's a lot of work, like cleaning the tub, where mold begins to grow back as soon as she's done.

"It's Christmas," my mom said, pushing me into the car. "We always clean you up for a holiday." The look on her face said that if my mold started to grow back before we got to our destination, I could forget about seeing another holiday.

Then before I knew it, we were getting out of our car and everyone started marching toward an old gray building that looked like—yikes!!!—a school!

What could be worse than going to school on Christmas Day?

Going to an *all-girls* school/orphanage, that's what.

But it was too late.

I walked straight into a roomful of girls!

"*Ni men hao*," they greeted us.

Then they sang us a couple of Christmas songs in Chinese. I had no idea what they sang, but it sure sounded like "Silent Night" and "We Wish You a Merry Christmas."

After that, the teacher said something in Chinese that sounded like the girls were excited to have visitors and that we should help ourselves to dried plums and dates and red bean cakes and tea, which she really didn't have to say on account of my dad was already helping himself. He loves Chinese treats.

Normally, I love Chinese treats too. But this was not normal. These treats came with a bunch of *girls,* who surrounded me. And the problem with girls, as everyone knows, is that they're not boys. They talk too much. They wear dresses. They put stuff on your plate. They want to hold your hand.

Oh brother.

Then Katie announced that there were presents for all.

"The gifts appeared overnight," Katie said excitedly.

"It's a miracle!" Bean Sprout cried. "It's a miracle!"

"I knew something fantastic like this would happen," Katie said. Then she turned to me and said, "You're very thoughtful, Alvin."

Then Katie hugged me with her eyes, which is the best kind of hug to get from a girl, if she's going to hug you anyway. No cooties!

"Yeah, your wrapping job isn't great, but you did a good thing, little bro," Calvin said.

"Look how happy you made everyone!" Anibelly cried. "Have you ever seen so many people so happy?"

I looked.

All the grown-ups were smiling and talking

in a corner of the room. All the orphans were playing with their new toys.

Anibelly was right. Everyone was very happy.

Everyone but me.

I was still holding the "friend" ornament.

Worse, there was a girl, about my size, who didn't get a gift.

Gulp.

Like I said, I always get the girl.

"Ni hao?" she said, when she saw that I was holding the ornament.

I froze.

My mom had taught me to say *"Ni hao?"* last night, which means "How are you?" in Chinese. But I said nothing.

The girl smiled.

Was I supposed to smile back? I couldn't remember.

"Wo jiao Emily," she said.

That didn't sound too Chinese. But I clutched my PDK anyway.

Emily pointed to my PDK.

"Shenma?" she asked.

I opened it and grabbed the stress balls. Boy, was I glad I had them! They are two shiny metal balls that you hold in your hands when you're stressed. Hit them together and all your stress will be gone, like magic.

ClackClack. I hit them together.

Nothing happened.

ClackClack. I hit them again.

Emily was still standing there. She had not disappeared.

Maybe I was supposed to clack them on her!

The look on her face said I'd better not try, or else! Lucky for me, I had something else in my PDK.

My yo-yo and string.

I put away the stress balls.

I put my yo-yo on the string.

Clunk. My yo-yo landed on the floor.

The yo-yo dude made it look so easy. He did lots of tricks. He was very impressive.

But I was not.

Worse, Emily picked up my yo-yo, and it did a bunch of tricks for her. No fair!

Then she said a bunch of Chinese words that sounded like she could teach me the tricks.

So she did.

It was super-duper! I needed a lot of practice. But practicing with Emily was really fun, sort of.

It felt like I had made a friend. She hadn't run away screaming at the top of her lungs. And I hadn't either.

But the problem with being friends with a girl, Calvin told me, is that you have to impress her more than she's impressed you, or you're in trouble.

So I looked in my PDK again.

Nothing.

All I needed was a jawbreaker to show her I could crack it with my teeth, or a pen to show her I could write.

I checked my jacket pockets.

Nothing.

I poked in my secret hiding place (my socks).

Nothing.

I reached into my back pants pocket.

Something.

I pulled it out.

It was warm.

And flat.

And blue.

"'Passport,'" I read aloud, carefully. "'United States of America.'"

Reading is very impressive.

GASP!!!

What was my *passport* doing in my pants pocket? I thought my dad was safekeeping it in his fanny pack.

I opened it.

GASSSSSSP!!!!!

The photo looked nothing like me.

Not one bit.

But it sure looked a lot like my dad.

Oops.

Whose passport was that little blue ball???

Alvin Ho's
Strangely Foreign Glossary

acupuncture— Chinese medicine. A way of healing you by turning you into a human pincushion.

Air Quality Index (AQI)— Tells you how clean or polluted the air is, on a scale of 0 to 500.

anthrax— A disease caused by a bacteria that is breathed, eaten or absorbed into the body through a cut in the skin. Looks like a cold, then the flu, then you die.

Bean Sprout— My cousin who's as small as a bean sprout and as strong as a crowbar.

Beijing— The capital of China.

Buddhist monks— Dudes who work in a Buddhist temple. They can do kung fu, write fancy Chinese calligraphy and sit still for ten minutes straight.

chi— The Chinese word for "energy" or "breath."

China— aka the People's Republic of China (PRC). Home of pandas, dinosaurs, kung fu monks, and 1.35 billion people! Birthplace of explosions, kites, compasses, seismographs, chopsticks, tea, writing, paper, printing presses, books!

China Art Museum in Shanghai— A huge building full of Chinese treasures from the past and present. It looks like a giant Chinese character. Admission is free!

chopsticks— Two thin sticks used for spearing food and putting it in your mouth. May be lethal if you miss.

coimetrophobia— Fear of cemeteries.

Community Party— The people in charge of China.

embassy— You need to go here if you lose your passport or if you get busted in another country.

eunuch— Look it up in the dictionary.

fanny pack— A kind of purse that tourists strap around their middle for holding valuables.

Fa Xian— A Chinese Buddhist monk who went to India between 394 and 414 in search of real Buddhist writings. He and his friends stopped at many of the sacred sites that the Buddha had stopped at.

Forbidden City— The palace and home of Chinese emperors from 1420 to 1911, located in the center of Beijing and surrounded by a tall wall. It could take you forever to walk through all of its 980 buildings. But if you skip most of them, like I did, and spend most of the morning in the bathroom, you could get through the tour in just a couple of hours.

fortune-teller— Someone who can tell you what your dusty life map looks like, either by looking at your face or by looking at the time, place and date of your birth.

g-force— Gravitational force.

Great Wall of China— 1. A construction project that took forever to finish. Actually, they never really finished it—it's built in sections, with large gaps between some of the sections. 2. Built to keep out invaders from the north (Mongols), but they came through anyway. See *Mongols* and *Yuan dynasty*. 3. Looks like a long dragon stretched out on the mountain ridge for as far as the eye can see.

GungGung— My grandpa; my mom's dad. He knows a lot of stuff about China.

hung bau— A red envelope filled with money and given to children on holidays and birthdays, or for no special reason at all!

hutong— Alleys and narrow streets of the old neighborhoods in Beijing. Rhymes with "oolong."

kung fu— A Chinese fighting method that is very cool and takes years to learn.

Lantian Man— Lived half a million to a million years ago in China. Older than the Peking man, but was not a man. The fossils are probably two females. Buried close by were pebbles and ashes, which meant people back then had tools and could control fire.

Mao Zedong— aka Chairman Mao. Founder of the People's Republic of China. His mummied body is in a creepy building in Tiananmen Square.

Marco Polo— 1. An explorer from Venice who traveled to Asia with his father and uncle in 1271, when he was seventeen. The trip took twenty-four years. It's possible that afterward, Marco Polo introduced noodles from China to Italy. 2. A game played at the pool.

Ming dynasty— Ruled China from 1368 to 1644. Built the Forbidden City and parts of the Great Wall. Eunuchs became very powerful during this time. Inventions of the time include novels written for common people to read, a two-colored printing process and the bristle toothbrush.

Mongols— 1. People of Mongolia. 2. Includes the khans, who ruled China during the Yuan dynasty from 1271 to 1368.

Mount Everest— The tallest mountain peak in the world, at 8,848 meters (29,029 feet) above sea level. Located in the Himalayas in Nepal.

Mutianyu— A village containing a large section of the Great Wall, about two hours from Beijing. Mutianyu was likely established by the soldiers guarding this section of the wall.

Mütter Museum— Located in Philadelphia, it contains mummified body parts and Siamese twins.

panda— aka giant panda. A black and white bear native to China. It lives mostly in the mountains in Sichuan province. Its diet is 99 percent bamboo. For a small fee, you can hold a baby panda at the Chengdu Research Base of Giant Panda Breeding.

passport— 1. The United States passport is a blue book with your photo in it. Used for get-

ting stamps and visas when you travel abroad.
2. Used for getting back into your own country.
3. Will turn into a little blue ball if it goes through the laundry.

PDK— Personal Disaster Kit, filled with emergency supplies for Peking, the old name for Beijing.

Peeking duck— A yummy treat with pancakes and duck sauce. Dip your chopstick into the duck sauce, draw a duck peeking at you on your pancake. Roll it up and eat it!

Peking Man— Found near Beijing, these old dudes (and ladies) lived 500,000 to 300,000 years ago. A bunch of stone tools were buried nearby, which meant that these Peking guys were the first builders of tools.

PohPoh— My grandma; my mom's mom. Makes lots of yummy things to eat.

Qin Shi Huang (259 BC–210 BC)— The first emperor of a unified China in 221 BC. He started construction of the Great Wall. He built the terra-cotta army to guard his tomb. He didn't actually do these things himself; he forced a lot of people to do it for him. Millions died working on his projects.

sampot— Worn in Cambodia, it's a long, rectangular cloth that ties around the waist and reaches down to the ankles.

SARS— Severe Acute Respiratory Syndrome. A virus that you can catch by breathing. Looks like a cold, then the flu, then you're dead. It killed a bunch of people in Hong Kong in 2003, and people there are still deathly afraid of it.

terra-cotta army— More than 8,000 warriors made of clay, along with their chariots, horses and weapons, were buried in the tomb of China's first emperor, Qin Shi Huang, in Xi'an. Each warrior has different facial features and expressions, probably based on an actual soldier. The terra-cotta army was built to protect the emperor in the afterlife.

Tiananmen Square— A large open area in the center of Beijing. It is one of the largest city centers in the world. There are no trees anywhere.

turbulence— Unstable airflow that makes a plane go up and down and shake like crazy. Then the pilot will tell you that he's turned on the seat belt sign, which is really a sign that you should say your prayers.

visa— A permit that goes inside your passport that allows you to get into a country.

Xuanzang— A Chinese Buddhist monk who lived from 602 to 664. He traveled to India to study the Buddhist scriptures, many of which he translated into Chinese. Also known for his writings about his travels.

YehYeh— My grandpa; my dad's dad. Lives in his family village in southern China for part of the year.

Yuan dynasty— 1271–1368. Established by Kublai Khan, who invaded China from Mongolia.

He gave Marco Polo a job as an official. It was the first dynasty to use paper money. See *Mongols*.

Zheng He— a famous eunuch who led seven epic sea voyages from 1405 to 1433 during the Ming dynasty. His expeditions involved hundreds of huge ships and tens of thousands of sailors and other passengers. His largest ships (more than 60 on his first voyage of 317 ships) were more than 400 feet long and 160 feet wide, with 9 masts and 12 sails, several stories and luxurious staterooms with balconies. He went all the way to India, the Persian Gulf and the east coast of Africa. No one since has led ocean expeditions as far or as large.

Zhucheng— Chinese city that is home of the world's largest dinosaur pit. You can walk right through the pit and see dinosaurs buried one on top of another, like dinosaur pie. Located in Shandong province, the city has at least thirty excavation sites. Locals used to make medicine by grinding the bones into powder.

Lenore Look is the author of the popular Alvin Ho series, as well as the Ruby Lu series. She has also written several acclaimed picture books, including *Henry's First-Moon Birthday, Uncle Peter's Amazing Chinese Wedding,* and *Brush of the Gods.* Lenore lives in Hoboken, New Jersey.

LeUyen Pham is the illustrator of the Alvin Ho series, as well as *The Best Birthday Party Ever* by Jennifer LaRue Huget; *Grace for President* by Kelly DiPucchio, a *New York Times* bestseller; and the Freckleface Strawberry series by Julianne Moore. She is the author and illustrator of the picture books *Big Sister, Little Sister* and *All the Things I Love About You.* LeUyen lives in San Francisco. Learn more at leuyenpham.com.

Afraid you've missed one of the Alvin Ho books?
Fear no more!

Alvin Ho: Allergic to Girls, School,
and Other Scary Things

Alvin Ho: Allergic to Camping,
Hiking, and Other Natural Disasters

Alvin Ho: Allergic to Birthday Parties,
Science Projects, and Other
Man-Made Catastrophes

Alvin Ho: Allergic to Dead Bodies, Funerals,
and Other Fatal Circumstances

Alvin Ho: Allergic to Babies, Burglars,
and Other Bumps in the Night

Alvin Ho: Allergic to the Great Wall,
the Forbidden Palace, and
Other Tourist Attractions